THE HAT THAT ZACK LOVES

PUFFIN

Michelle Robinson

illustrated by Robert Reader

This is the HAT
that Zack loves.

This is the **shop** that sells
the **HAT** that Zack loves.

This is the **dog** that *races past*
And snatches
the **HAT** that Zack loves.

This is the way the dog *runs*.
Down the sidewalk.
WHOOSH! Through the dark!
A ride on the subway,

Then into the park
To play with
the HAT that Zack loves.

This is the **cat** the dog sees.

This is the *wind* that spooks the cat
And ruffles the dog,
 And **off** blows the **HAT!**
Up into the **tree**
 that Zack **climbs.**

This is the way that Zack falls.
Out of the tree
     And BUMP!
          to the ground
Right next to the lake
Where a grey goose has found
the HAT that Zack loves.

Away swims the goose
Along with the **HAT**
That *blew* from the tree
Right next to the cat

That was chased by the dog
That *raced past* the shop
And snatched
the **HAT** that Zack loves.

BOATS FOR HIRE

POPPY

DAIS

MOLLY

This is the **boat** the wind *blows.*
Across the lake,
S p L O S H !
Over the ridge.

Round the big fountain
         and under the bridge
Right after
         the **HAT** that Zack loves.

This is the way
    the wind *keeps blowing*,
And this is the way
    Zack's **HAT** is going...

Away from the goose
That found the HAT
That *blew* from the tree
Right next to the cat

That was chased by the dog
That *raced past* the shop
And snatched
the HAT that Zack loves.

This is the way the dog *runs*.

Over the road and after the **HAT**.
 He's ever so **sorry**
for upsetting Zack!

He'll get back
 the **HAT** that Zack loves.

Who's joined by the goose
That found the **HAT**
That *blew* from the tree
Right next to the cat

That was chased by the dog
That *raced past* the shop
And snatched
the **HAT** that Zack loves.

This is the place the **HAT** lands.
Up on a statue,
   watched by poor Zack.
It's well out of reach now,
   but Zack wants it **BACK!**

These are the friends
that help Zack.

A man and a horse,

A windswept cat,

A goose...

and a dog.

And at the TOP — Zack!

They wobble...

they STRETCH...

and they REACH...

Zack's HAT!

This is the HAT
that Zack loves!

These are the **friends**
that he loves the **BEST**.
The dog and the cat and all of the rest
Who saved
the **HAT** that Zack loves.

Meeting them **all** has
been **so** much **FUN,**

Now it's back to the shop
to buy everyone one.

That was the HAT that Zack loves!

For Isaac Stapleton – M. R.

For Marni, my little artist – R. R.

PUFFIN BOOKS
UK | USA | Canada | Ireland | Australia | India | New Zealand | South Africa
Puffin Books is part of the Penguin Random House group of companies
whose addresses can be found at global.penguinrandomhouse.com.
www.penguin.co.uk   www.puffin.co.uk   www.ladybird.co.uk

 Penguin
Random House
UK

First published 2017   001
Text copyright © Michelle Robinson, 2017
Illustrations copyright © Robert Reader, 2017
The moral right of the author and illustrator has been asserted
Printed in China
A CIP catalogue record for this book is available from the British Library
ISBN: 978–0–141–37967–8
All correspondence to: Puffin Books, Penguin Random House Children's
80 Strand, London WC2R 0RL